Let's Play Tag!

- Read the Page
- Read the Story
- Repeat
- Stop

- Game
- Yes
- No

TO USE THIS BOOK WITH THE TAG™ READER you must download audio from the LeapFrog Connect application. The LeapFrog Connect application can be installed from the CD provided with your Tag Reader or at leapfrog.com/tag.

OLIVIA

written and illustrated by Ian Falconer

This is Olivia.
She is good at lots of things.

She is *very* good at wearing people out.

She even wears herself out.

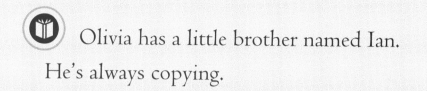 Olivia has a little brother named Ian.
He's always copying.

Sometimes Ian just won't leave her alone,
so Olivia has to be firm.

Olivia lives with her mother, her father, her brother, her dog, Perry,

and Edwin, the cat.

In the morning, after she gets up,
and moves the cat,

and brushes her teeth,
and combs her ears,

and moves the cat,

 Olivia gets dressed.

She has to try on everything.

On sunny days, Olivia likes to go to the beach.

She feels it's important
to come prepared.

Last summer when Olivia was little,
her mother showed her how to make sand castles.

She got pretty good.

Sometimes Olivia likes
to bask in the sun.

When her mother sees that she's had
enough, they go home.

Every day Olivia is supposed to take a nap.

"It's time for your you-know-what,"
her mother says.

Of course Olivia's not at all sleepy.

On rainy days, Olivia likes to go to the museum.

She heads straight for her favorite picture.

Olivia looks at it for a long time.

What could she be thinking?

 But there is one painting Olivia just doesn't get.
"I could do that in about five minutes,"
she says to her mother.

As soon as she gets home she gives it a try.

Time out.

After a nice bath,

and a nice dinner,

it's time for bed.

But of course Olivia's not at all sleepy.

"Only five books tonight, Mommy," she says.

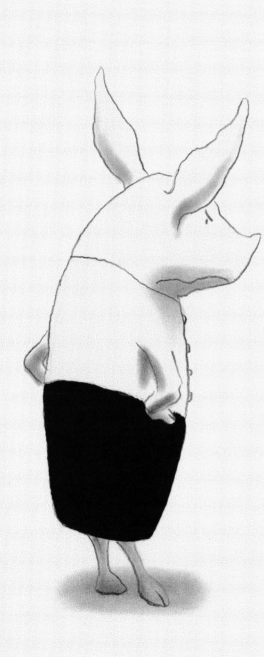

"No, Olivia, just one."

"How about four?"

"Two."

"Three."

"Oh, all right, three.
But that's *it!*"

When they've finished reading, Olivia's mother gives her a kiss and says, "You know, you really wear me out. But I love you anyway." And Olivia gives her a kiss back and says, "I love you anyway too."

To the real Olivia and Ian,
and to William,
who didn't arrive in time to appear in this book.